All on a Sleepy Night

Story by Shutta Crum
Illustrations by Sylvie Daigneault

Stoddart
Kids
TORONTO • NEW YORK

Published in Canada in 2001 by
Stoddart Kids,
a division of Stoddart Publishing Co. Limited
895 Don Mills Road, 400-2 Park Centre
Toronto, Ontario M3C 1W3
Tel (416) 445-3333 Fax (416) 445-5967
E-mail cservice@genpub.com

Distributed in Canada by
General Distribution Services
325 Humber College Blvd.,
Toronto, ON M9W 7C3
Tel (416) 213-1919 Fax (416) 213-1917
E-mail cservice@genpub.com

Published in the United States in 2002 by
Stoddart Kids,
a division of Stoddart Publishing Co. Limited
180 Varick Street, 9th Floor
New York, New York 10014
Toll free 1-800-805-1083
E-mail gdsinc@genpub.com

Distributed in the United States by
General Distribution Services
4500 Witmer Industrial Estates, PMB 128
Niagara Falls, New York 14305-1386
Toll free 1-800-805-1083
E-mail gdsinc@genpub.com

Canadian Cataloguing in Publication Data

Crum, Shutta, 1951–
All on a sleepy night

ISBN 0-7737-3315-9

I. Daigneault, Sylvie. II. Title.

PZ7.C955A1 2001   j813'.6   C2001-930586-9

*All the night noises that surround a sleepy child
are explored in a comforting, musical poem.*

THE CANADA COUNCIL | LE CONSEIL DES ARTS
FOR THE ARTS | DU CANADA
SINCE 1957 | DEPUIS 1957

*We acknowledge for their financial support of our
publishing program the Canada Council, the Ontario Arts
Council, and the Government of Canada through the
Book Publishing Industry Development Program (BPIDP).*

Printed and bound in Hong Kong, China
by Book Art Inc., Toronto

For Sam,
Grandma's own sleepy boy.
— S.C.

For Ben's
sleepless nights.
— S.D.

In a little log house,
On a great green hill,
Under a shimmering sky;

One small boy,
On his grandparents' bed,
Whispers "goodnight" with a sigh.

Mandu and Max are lying there too,
And they begin to purr.
Down on the rug, thumping his tail,
Buck dreams of the wind in his fur.

Purr, thump, purr, thump,
All on a sleepy night.
Purr, thump, purr, thump,
Under a northern sky.

Grandma and Grandpa, in flowered pajamas,
Tiptoe into bed.
Grandma snores, and Grandpa whistles,
With his arms above his head.

Snore, whiss, snore, whiss,
All on a sleepy night.
Snore, whiss, snore, whiss,
Under a northern sky.

Whimsey, the bird, who wants to be heard,
Makes himself known with a cry.
Ruffled up and ringing his bell,
He twitters a grumpy reply.

Br-i-n-n-g, twit, br-i-n-n-g, twit,
All on a sleepy night.
Br-i-n-n-g, twit, br-i-n-n-g, twit,
Under a northern sky.

While one small boy,
On his grandparents' bed,
Sits rubbing his heavy eyes;
The house about him is singing —
Singing its sleepy song.

Out of the blue, the heat gurgles too,
As the pipes begin to fill.
And the floor creaks, as it often does,
When relaxing from the chill.

Gurgle, creak, gurgle, creak,
All on a sleepy night.
Gurgle, creak, gurgle, creak,
Under a northern sky.

The fridge joins in with a jump and a jig,
Humming a tune or two.
But the faucet — old faucet — slow drippy — slow —
Hasn't much to do.

Hum, drip, hum, d — r — i — p,
All on a sleepy night.
Hum, d — r — i — p, hum, d— r — i —
Under a northern sky.

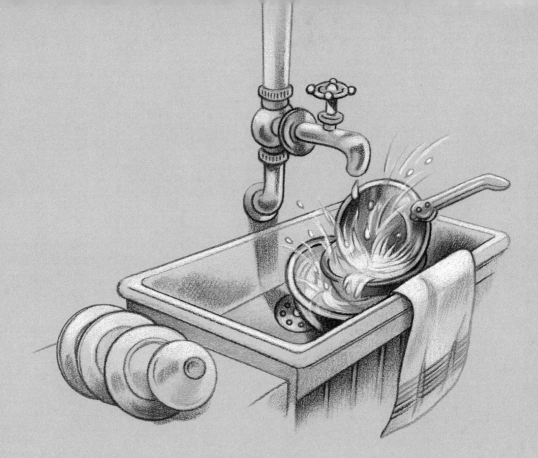

While one small boy,
On his grandparents' bed,
Yawns and stretches his arms;
The house about him is singing —
Singing its sleepy song.

Out on the road, the loggers and trucks
Go rumbling on their way.
And owls in the woods wonder aloud,
Who wants to stay up and play?

Rumble, who-o-o, rumble, who-o-o,
All on a sleepy night.
Rumble, who-o-o, rumble, who-o-o,
Under a northern sky.

Up on the ridge, a fox and her kits
Yip happily at the moon.
Down on the water, languid and long,
Echoes the cry of the loon.

Yip-ity yip; oo,oo, AH-hoo,
All on a sleepy night.
Yip-ity yip; oo,oo, AH-hoo,
Under a northern sky.

As little creatures that sleep in the dark
Whisper their soft goodnights,
The leaves on the trees sway in the breeze,
Beneath the northern lights.

Hush, swish, hush, swish,
All on a sleepy night.
Hush, swish, hush, swish,
Under a northern sky.

Now one small boy,
On his grandparents' bed,
Is asleep and dreaming along;

Under a shimmering sky —
High on a great green hill —
In a little log house that is singing,
Singing its sleepy song.